Rat Fair

Brooklyn, NY

WRITTEN BY LEAH ROSE KESSLER

ILLUSTRATED BY CLEONIQUE HILSACA

"To Ben and Elliot, for having the decency to not walk across my keyboard while I'm typing."—L.R.K.

"To Jesús, family, and friends, thank you for believing in me."—C.H.

Rat Fair

Text © 2021 Leah Rose Kessler
Images © 2021 Cleonique Hilsaca

Published in the United States by POW!
a division of powerHouse Packaging & Supply, Inc.
32 Adams Street, Brooklyn, NY 11201-1021

info@POWKidsBooks.com • www.POWKidsBooks.com • www.powerHouseBooks.com

First edition, 2021
Library of Congress Control Number: 2021931978

ISBN 978-1-57687-984-9

Printing and binding by Toppan Leefung

10 9 8 7 6 5 4 3 2 1

Printed in China